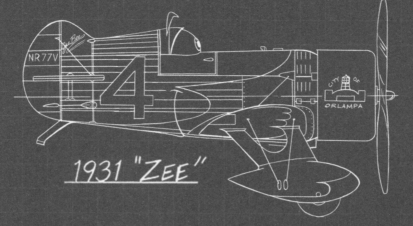

1931 "ZEE"

This book belongs to

_____

1933 "PUFF"

All of Life is a School

with

Gee Bee Zee - the Little Racer

Story, Concept & Characters by
Kermit Weeks

Illustrations by
Project Firefly artists
Ron Cohee
Robert Stanton
Artistic Coordinator
Pam Darley

Mia,
We all fly in our dreams!
I hope the Fantasy of Flight
helps light that Spark within

To Katie Anne
and
the potential
that lies within
us all!

A CHILDREN'S BOOK BY
KERMIT WEEKS
All of Life is a School Series

Library of Congress Control Number
2006910621

ISBN-10:0-9790267-0-9 ISBN-13:978-0-9790267-0-6

www.geebee.com
www.fantasyofflight.com

A long, long time ago, in a land of never ending summer,
there was a place, a very special place, called
Fantasy of Flight.

Fantasy of Flight was an airfield where many types of airplanes lived, each one special. To help push the boundaries of flight, the older and wiser planes would pass on their knowledge to the younger ones.

Journey now back in time, back to a place where all the planes reach beyond themselves and strive to become all they can be!

The friendly blue and gold biplane responds, "I'm Curtiss. And this is Benny. The girls over there . . . the red one's Missy, and the other one's Pancho."

Benny thinks for a moment and realizes, "Maybe you're right. Yeah, I think I'm going to like school!"

-7-

"Hello everyone. My name is Roscoe. Welcome to racing school. Today we will learn to fly safely around the race course."

PRE-FLIGHT
CHECKLIST ✓
- FUEL   - ON
- MIXTURE - RICH
- MAGNETOS - BOTH
- DOORS   - LOCKED
- LATCHES - LOCKED
- CONTROLS - FREE

Roscoe points to some clipboards and states in his best instructor voice, "I have some checklists I'd like to hand out before we go out to the practice area."

Still excited about Roscoe's comment, Zee proudly takes off.
Unfortunately, he FORGETS to use his checklist!

As the students finish up over the practice course, Roscoe yells, "OK, that's it for today. Let's see if you can find your way back to the airfield."

Missy and Pancho decide to buzz the airfield. They shout passing their landmark friends, "Hey Tether! Hey Checker!"

Surprised, they gasp, "You girls are sure looking good!"

Looking back at his friends, Zee yells, "Come on guys!
We can't let the girls show us up. Let's show
them what WE can do!"

Flying close together, Zee shouts, "OK, Ready, BREAK!"
Everyone yells with delight, "YIPPEE!"
as they pull up and zoom away.

Zee feels an immediate attraction to the charming Puff. Roscoe, on the other hand, is all business, "Puff, you'll have plenty of opportunity to catch up. Welcome to class!"

Zee tries to impress Puff and asks Roscoe, "Why do we have to use a checklist when we already know how to fly?"

At that point, Jimmy G. arrives. "Hello, Zee. How was class?" Changing the subject, Zee quickly chimes in, "Oh, hi Jimmy. These are some of my new friends."

He takes a bow, "Jimmy G. Gee Bee at your service, ladies!"
Zee notices that the girls are impressed and moves closer
to his big brother. He proudly announces, "And
WE'RE the Gee Bee Brothers!"

Wanting to impress Puff, Zee steps up and volunteers, "I'll do it!"
Jimmy is surprised, "Zee, you're plenty fast enough;
however, you've never flown that far from home."

Zee thinks for a moment before replying, "I'll let YOU help!"
Jimmy considers the offer, "I'll bet you could get some
extra credit for school. OK, WE'LL do it!"

Zee quickly finishes and starts rolling, "OK, I'm done!
Ready for take-off!" Before Jimmy can comment,
Zee roars off, "Come on Jimmy, let's go.
FOLLOW ME!!!!!!"

Jimmy replies, "Follow the railroad track . . . and it will take us to the State Capital!"

The next morning was quite cold at the State Capital Airfield. Jimmy reminds his brother, "Make sure you warm up your engine. You have the package, right?" Zee nods and proudly claims, "Yes . . . AND I looked at a map!"

Jimmy is delighted, but nevertheless asks, "Do you have your checklist?"
Zee fumbles around and says, "Oh, well, yes. It's here somewhere."

Zee finally produces his checklist. Again, he mumbles through it quickly. Before Jimmy can respond, Zee takes off down the runway.

As Jimmy pulls up from behind, Zee is full of confidence. "Hey Jimmy, where have you been? We'll never get that package delivered on time with you straggling behind!"

Arriving at Fantasy of Flight, Zee's friends gather to greet him and learn about his experience.

His friends ask in anticipation, "Did you get the package?" With confidence, Zee proudly replies, "Oh yeah, no problem. It's right . . ." Zee reaches for his baggage door and discovers it's open!

Embarrassed, Zee accepts the package from his big brother . . . and humbly departs.

not

The

End . . .

only

the

beginning . . .

FANTASY OF FLIGHT IS A REAL PLACE!

Did you know the characters in this book were real airplanes? Zee and his friends became famous during the Golden Age of Aviation. Many of them live at Fantasy of Flight in Central Florida. It's a fun place to play where everyone loves to learn and grow.

MEET KERMIT

Hi, I'm Kermit and I created Fantasy of Flight as a place for all my airplane friends to come and play with me. Since I was a kid, I've loved flight and had big dreams.

I built my first airplane when I was eight years old, put it on my toy wagon, and rode down the street. It didn't really fly, but it never stopped me from dreaming.

As I grew up, I built three airplanes that did fly and have collected many more. I have always pursued my dreams and continue to do so. Find out what you love to do and then follow yours!

fantasy of flight™

An Attraction on a Higher Plane

Polk County (Orlampa), Florida

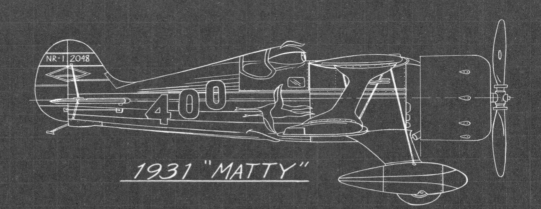

1931 "MATTY"

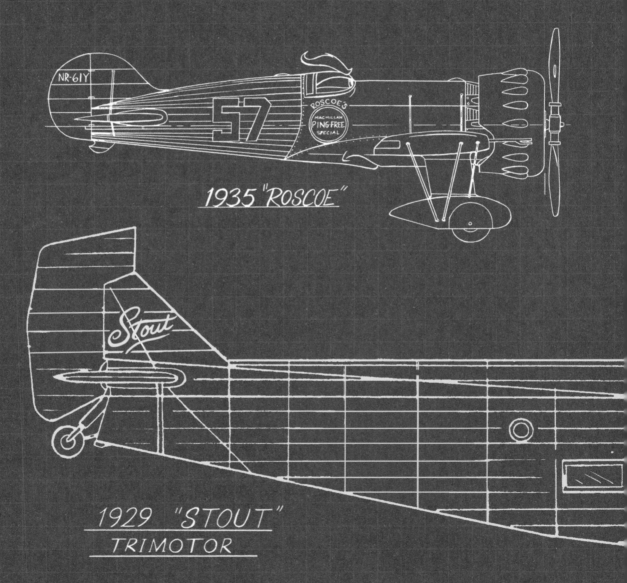

1935 "ROSCOE"

1929 "STOUT"
TRIMOTOR